The Big Pancake

retold by Elizabeth Rogers

Illustrated by Silvia Provantini

FRANKLIN WATTS
LONDON•SYDNEY

First published in 2009 by
Franklin Watts
338 Euston Road
London
NW1 3BH

Franklin Watts Australia
Level 17/207 Kent Street
Sydney
NSW 2000

A CIP catalogue record for this book is available
from the British Library.

ISBN 978 0 7496 8609 3 (hbk)
ISBN 978 0 7496 8615 4 (pbk)

Series Editor: Jackie Hamley
Series Advisor: Dr Barrie Wade
Series Designer: Peter Scoulding

Printed in China

Franklin Watts is a division of
Hachette Children's Books,
an Hachette UK company.
www.hachette.co.uk

Once there was a woman
who had seven children.

4

She made them
a big pancake and
her children shouted,
"Yum-yum! We want to
eat that big pancake!"

"They'll not eat me!"
cried the pancake.

It flipped out of the pan
and rolled away.

8

"Stop, pancake!
My children want to eat
you!" shouted the woman.
But the pancake said,
"I won't stop for you."
It rolled away.

Soon an old man
saw the pancake.
"Stop, pancake! I want
to eat you!" he cried.

11

12

But the pancake said, "I didn't stop for the woman, or the seven children. I won't stop for you!" It rolled away.

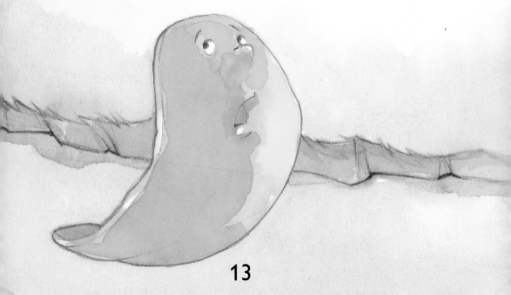

Next a hen saw
the pancake.

"Stop, pancake! I want to eat you!" she clucked.

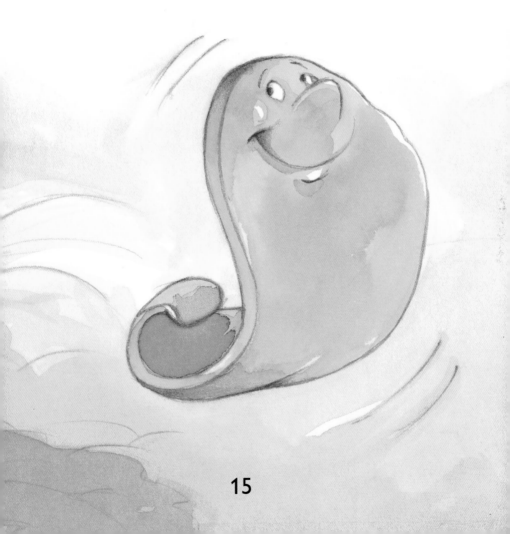

But the pancake said,
"I didn't stop for the
woman, or the seven
children, or the old man.
I won't stop for you!"
It rolled away.

Then a dog saw
the pancake.
"Stop, pancake!
I want to eat you!"
he barked.

19

But the
pancake said,

"I didn't stop for
the woman or the
seven children,
or the old man,
or the hen.

I won't stop for you!"
It rolled away.

21

A hungry pig was
by a stream and
he saw the pancake.
"Stop, pancake! Can
you cross the stream?"
the pig grunted.

"No, I can't swim,"
said the pancake.

"Get on my snout and
I will swim across
with you," the
pig grunted.

The pancake rolled on
to the pig's snout.
"You're a yummy pancake!"
the pig grunted ...

27

... and he ate it up!

Puzzle 1

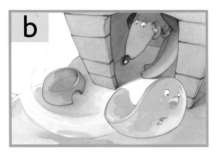

Put these pictures in the correct order.
Now tell the story in your own words.
What different endings can you think of?

Puzzle 2

slow   fast

angry

greedy   clever

silly

busy   surprised

frightened

Choose the correct adjectives for each character. Which adjectives are incorrect? Turn over to find the answers.

Answers

Puzzle 1

The correct order is: 1c, 2f, 3e, 4b, 5a, 6d

Puzzle 2

Pancake: the correct adjective is fast

The incorrect adjectives are angry, slow

Pig: the correct adjectives are clever, greedy

The incorrect adjective is silly

Woman: the correct adjectives are busy, surprised

The incorrect adjective is frightened

Look out for Leapfrog fairy tales:

Cinderella
ISBN 978 0 7496 4228 0

The Three Little Pigs
ISBN 978 0 7496 4227 3

Jack and the Beanstalk
ISBN 978 0 7496 4229 7

The Three Billy Goats Gruff
ISBN 978 0 7496 4226 6

Goldilocks and the Three Bears
ISBN 978 0 7496 4225 9

Little Red Riding Hood
ISBN 978 0 7496 4224 2

Rapunzel
ISBN 978 0 7496 6159 5

Snow White
ISBN 978 0 7496 6161 8

The Emperor's New Clothes
ISBN 978 0 7496 6163 2

The Pied Piper of Hamelin
ISBN 978 0 7496 6164 9

Hansel and Gretel
ISBN 978 0 7496 6162 5

The Sleeping Beauty
ISBN 978 0 7496 6160 1

Rumpelstiltskin
ISBN 978 0 7496 6165 6

The Ugly Duckling
ISBN 978 0 7496 6166 3

Puss in Boots
ISBN 978 0 7496 6167 0

The Frog Prince
ISBN 978 0 7496 6168 7

The Princess and the Pea
ISBN 978 0 7496 6169 4

Dick Whittington
ISBN 978 0 7496 6170 0

The Little Match Girl
ISBN 978 0 7496 6582 1

The Elves and the Shoemaker
ISBN 978 0 7496 6581 4

The Little Mermaid
ISBN 978 0 7496 6583 8

The Little Red Hen
ISBN 978 0 7496 6585 2

The Nightingale
ISBN 978 0 7496 6586 9

Thumbelina
ISBN 978 0 7496 6587 6

The Magic Porridge Pot
ISBN 978 0 7496 8605 5*
ISBN 978 0 7496 8611 6

The Enormous Turnip
ISBN 978 0 7496 8606 2*
ISBN 978 0 7496 8612 3

Chicken Licken
ISBN 978 0 7496 8607 9*
ISBN 978 0 7496 8613 0

The Three Wishes
ISBN 978 0 7496 8608 6*
ISBN 978 0 7496 8614 7

The Big Pancake
ISBN 978 0 7496 8609 3*
ISBN 978 0 7496 8615 4

The Gingerbread Man
ISBN 978 0 7496 8610 9*
ISBN 978 0 7496 8616 1

* hardback